W9-BZY-038

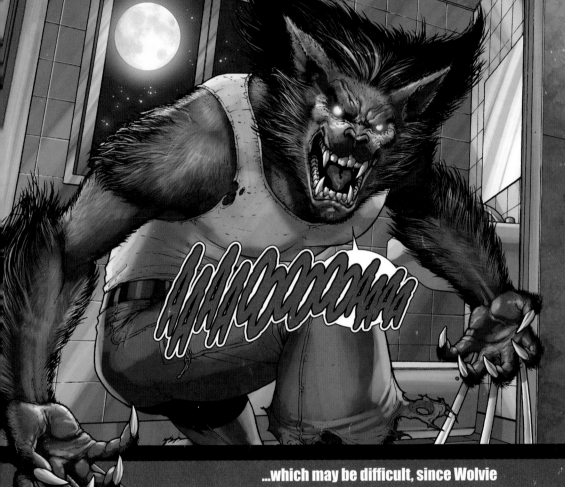

ty Pryde wants to become one of the mutant super hero X-Men. But she'll have to survive as the original member of

WOLVERINE
FIRST CLASS

...which may be difficult, since Wolvie just got bit by a love-struck werewolf.

(Werewolves don't make good teachers.)

THE PACK part 2

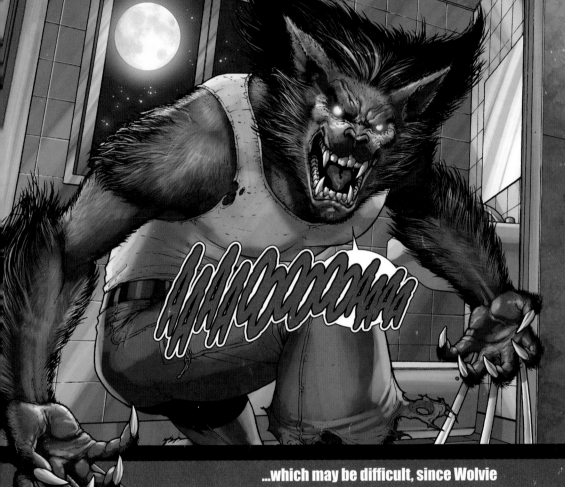

WRITTEN BY
FRED VAN LENTE

ART BY
HUGO PETRUS

COLORED BY
ULISES ARREOLA

LETTERED BY
VC'S JOE CARAMAGNA

COVER BY
WILLIAMS & QUINTANA

PAUL ACERIOS
PRODUCTION

RALPH MACCHIO
CONSULTING

NATHAN COSBY
EDITOR

JOE QUESADA
EDITOR IN CHIEF

DAN BUCKLEY
PUBLISHER

MARVEL

Spotlight

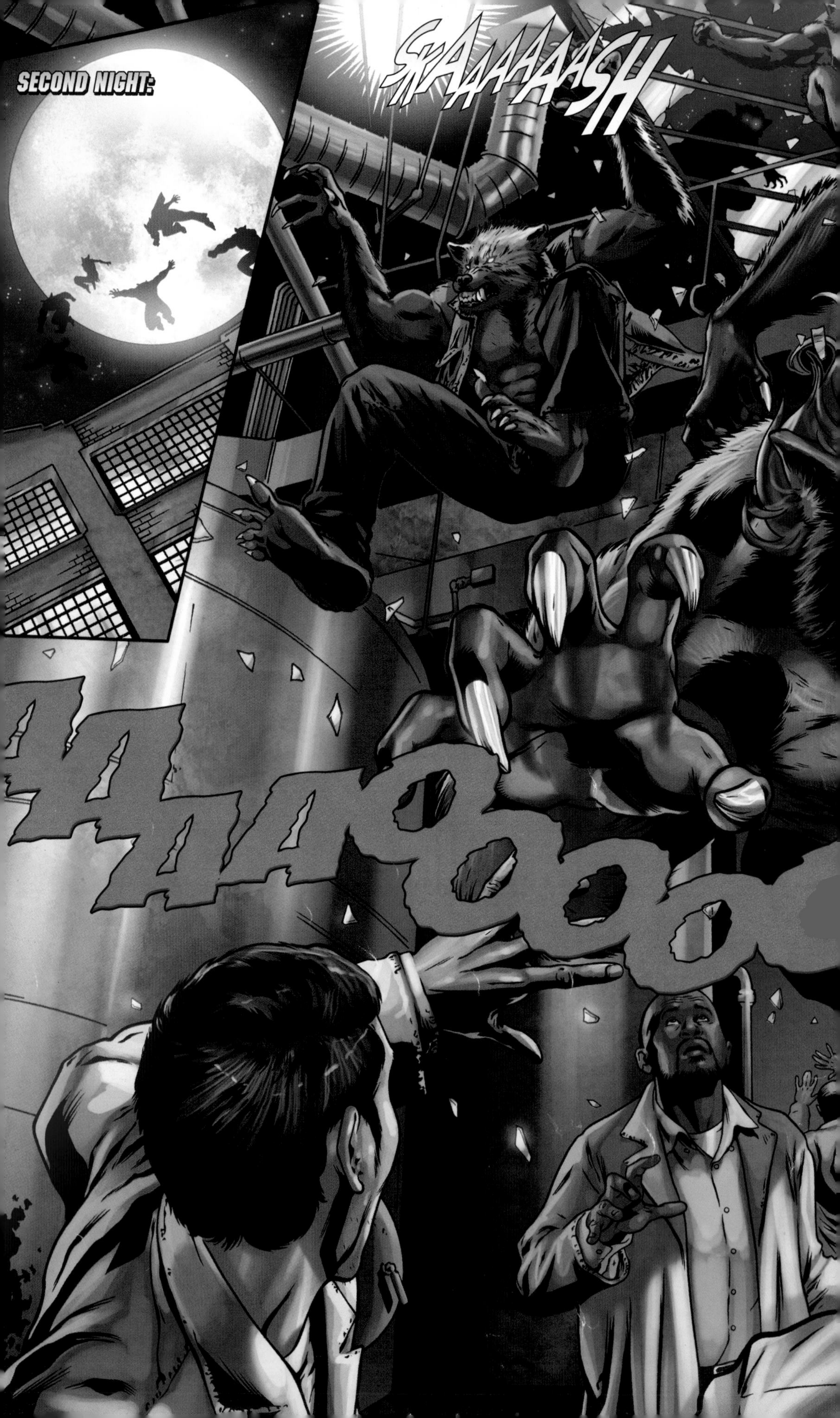
SECOND NIGHT:
SKAAAAAAASH
HAROOO

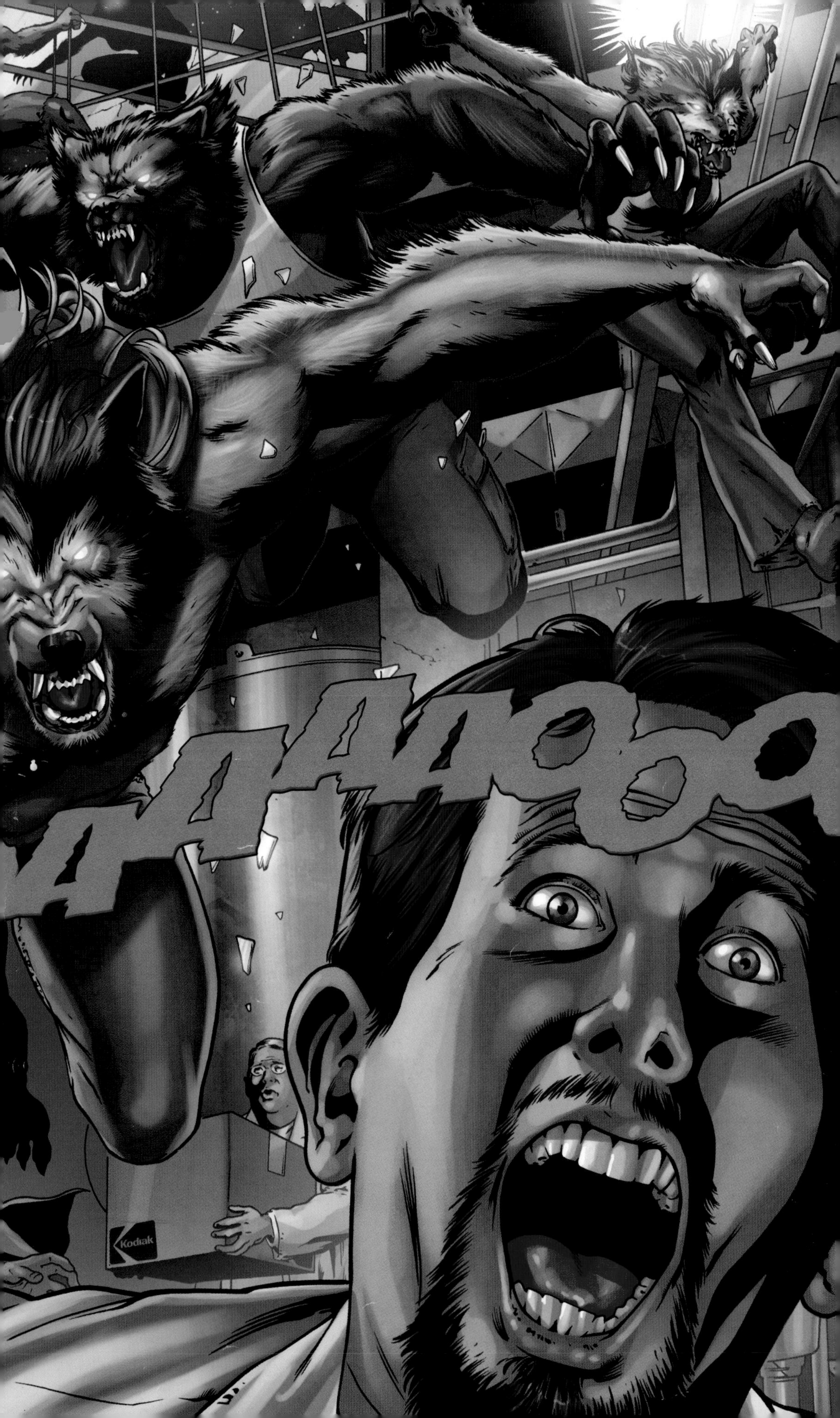
AAHOOO
Kodiak

Visit us at www.abdopublishing.com

Reinforced library bound editions published in 2014 by Spotlight, a division of the ABDO Group, PO Box 398166, Minneapolis, MN 55439. Spotlight produces high-quality reinforced library bound editions for schools and libraries. Published by agreement with Marvel Characters, Inc.

Printed in the United States of America, North Mankato, Minnesota.
042013
092013
♻ This book contains at least 10% recycled material.

marvel.com
© 2013 Marvel

Library of Congress Cataloging-in-Publication Data

Van Lente, Fred
 [Graphic novels. Selections]
 The pack / story by Fred Van Lente ; art by Francis Portela. -- Reinforced library bound edition.
     volumes cm. -- (Wolverine, first class)
 "Marvel."
 Summary: "Wolverine's claws and healing factor have helped him survive some of the most dangerous situations and locales. But what happens when dark magic transforms him into a werewolf?"-- Provided by publisher.
 ISBN 978-1-61479-178-2 (part 1) -- ISBN 978-1-61479-179-9 (part 2)
 1. Graphic novels. [1. Graphic novels. 2. Superheroes--Fiction.] I. Portela, Francis, illustrator. II. Title.
 PZ7.7.V26Pac 2013
 741.5'352--dc23
                                    2013005934

All Spotlight books are reinforced library bindings
and manufactured in the United States of America.

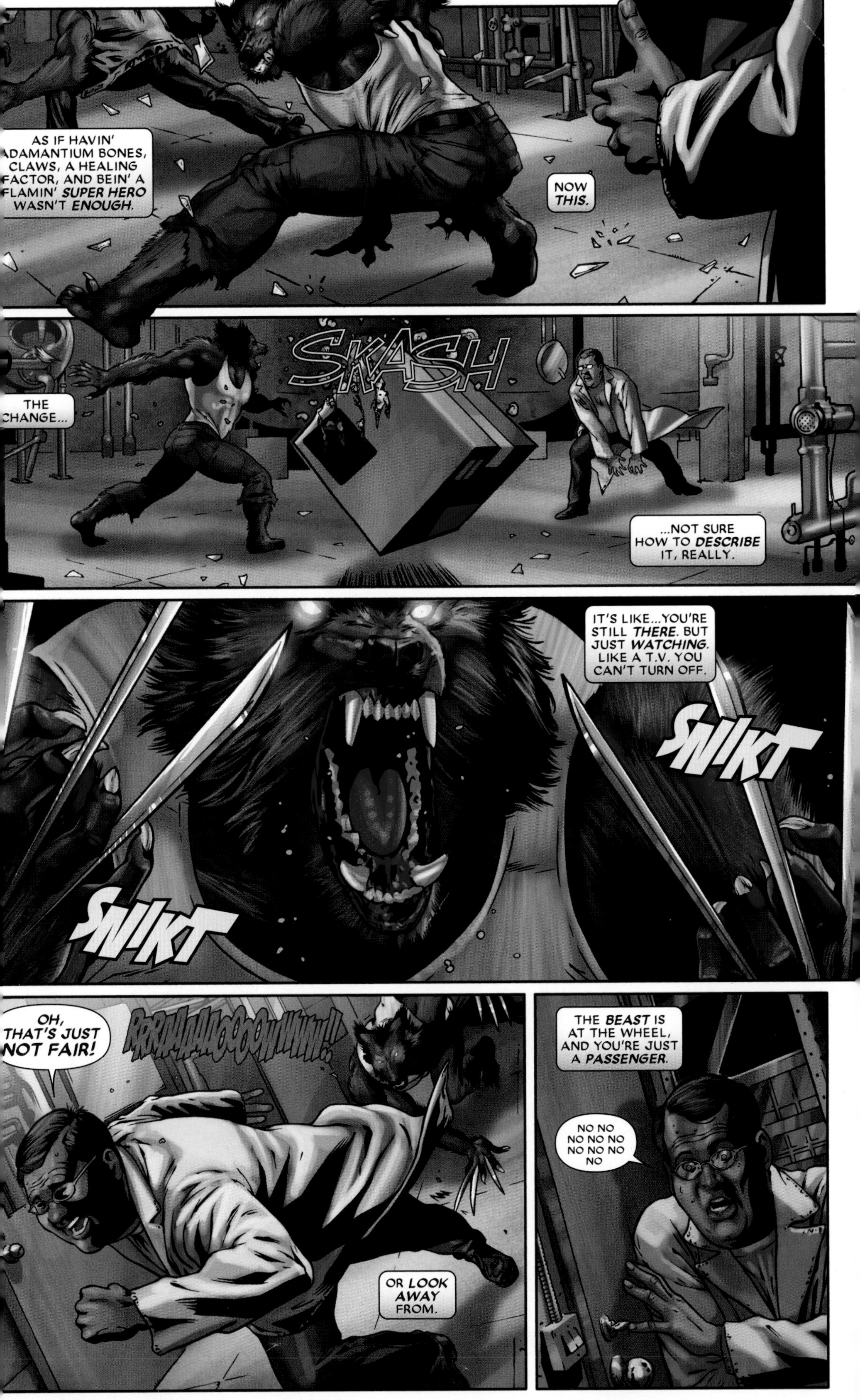
AS IF HAVIN' ADAMANTIUM BONES, CLAWS, A HEALING FACTOR, AND BEIN' A FLAMIN' SUPER HERO WASN'T ENOUGH.
NOW THIS.
SKASH
THE CHANGE...
...NOT SURE HOW TO DESCRIBE IT, REALLY.
IT'S LIKE...YOU'RE STILL THERE. BUT JUST WATCHING. LIKE A T.V. YOU CAN'T TURN OFF.
SNIKT
SNIKT
OH, THAT'S JUST NOT FAIR!
RRRAAAAOOOOWWWW!!
OR LOOK AWAY FROM.
THE BEAST IS AT THE WHEEL, AND YOU'RE JUST A PASSENGER.
NO NO NO NO NO NO NO NO NO

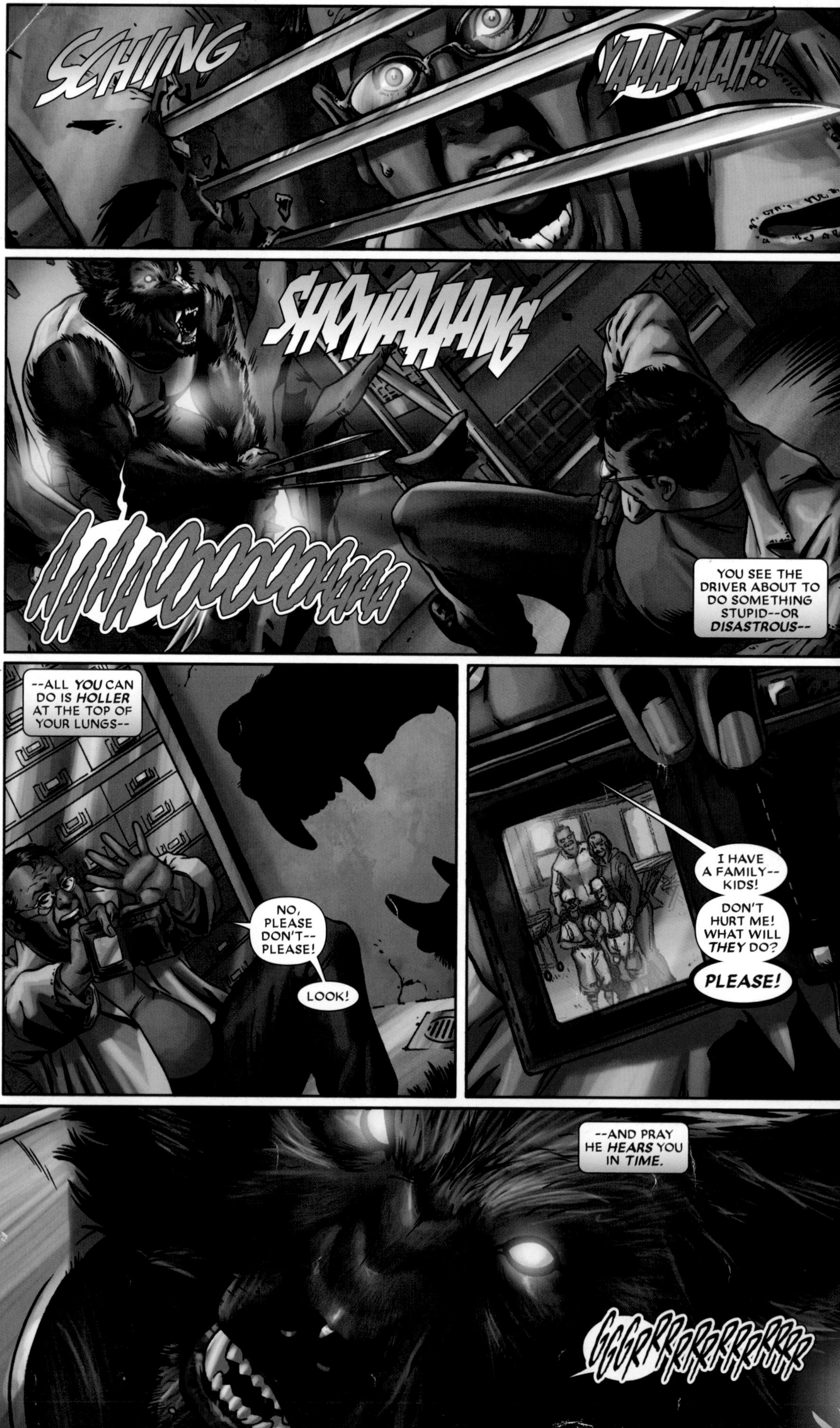
SCHIING
YAAAAAAH!!
SHOWAAAANG
AAAAOOOOOAAAA
YOU SEE THE DRIVER ABOUT TO DO SOMETHING STUPID--OR DISASTROUS--
--ALL YOU CAN DO IS HOLLER AT THE TOP OF YOUR LUNGS--
NO, PLEASE DON'T--PLEASE!
LOOK!
I HAVE A FAMILY--KIDS!
DON'T HURT ME! WHAT WILL THEY DO?
PLEASE!
--AND PRAY HE HEARS YOU IN TIME.
GGGRRRRRRRRRRRRR

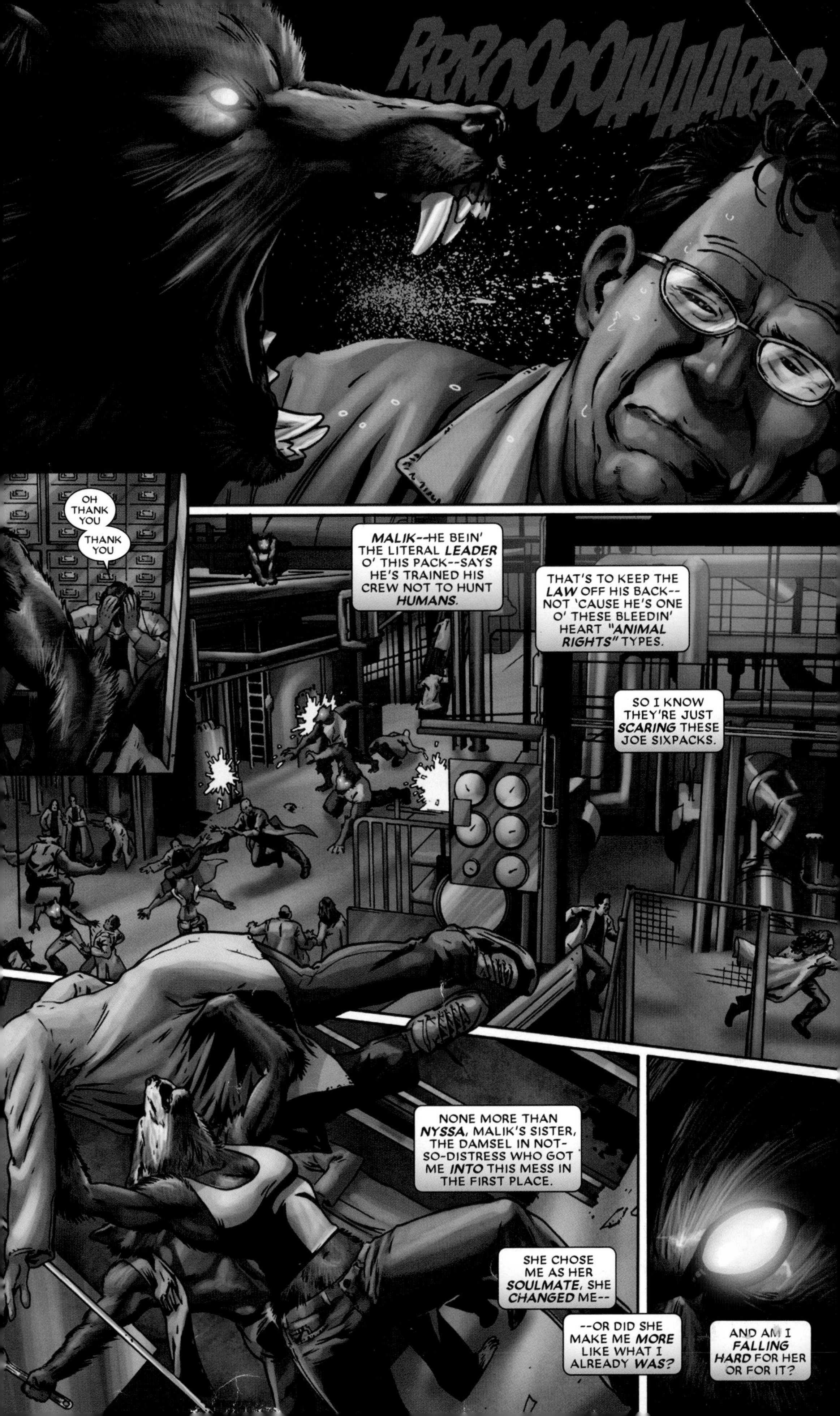

RRROOOOAAARRR
OH THANK YOU
THANK YOU
MALIK--HE BEIN' THE LITERAL LEADER O' THIS PACK--SAYS HE'S TRAINED HIS CREW NOT TO HUNT HUMANS.
THAT'S TO KEEP THE LAW OFF HIS BACK--NOT 'CAUSE HE'S ONE O' THESE BLEEDIN' HEART "ANIMAL RIGHTS" TYPES.
SO I KNOW THEY'RE JUST SCARING THESE JOE SIXPACKS.
NONE MORE THAN NYSSA, MALIK'S SISTER, THE DAMSEL IN NOT-SO-DISTRESS WHO GOT ME INTO THIS MESS IN THE FIRST PLACE.
SHE CHOSE ME AS HER SOULMATE, SHE CHANGED ME--
--OR DID SHE MAKE ME MORE LIKE WHAT I ALREADY WAS?
AND AM I FALLING HARD FOR HER OR FOR IT?

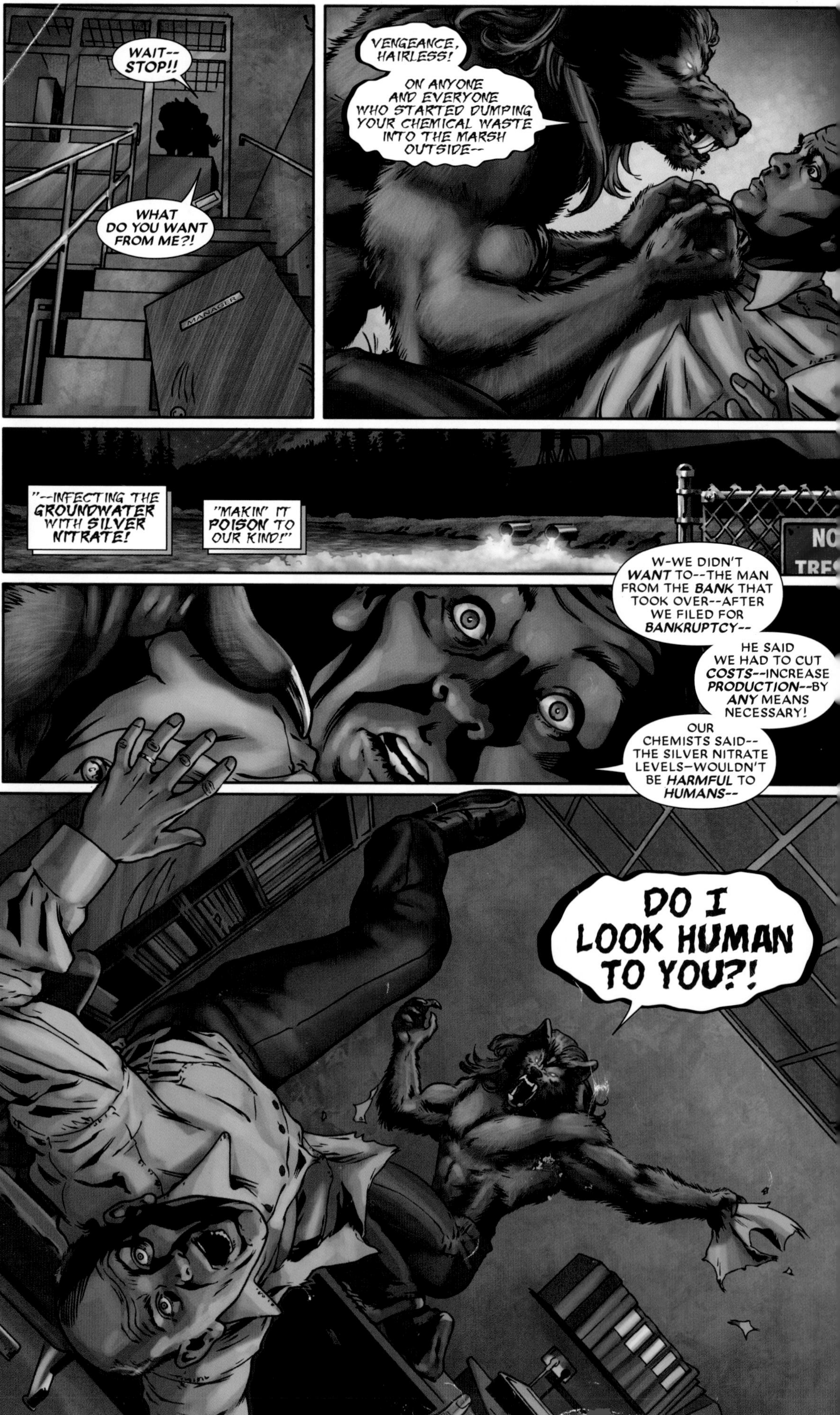
WAIT-- STOP!!
WHAT DO YOU WANT FROM ME?!
MANAGER
VENGEANCE, HAIRLESS!
ON ANYONE AND EVERYONE WHO STARTED DUMPING YOUR CHEMICAL WASTE INTO THE MARSH OUTSIDE--
"--INFECTING THE GROUNDWATER WITH SILVER NITRATE!
"MAKIN' IT POISON TO OUR KIND!"
NO
W-WE DIDN'T WANT TO--THE MAN FROM THE BANK THAT TOOK OVER--AFTER WE FILED FOR BANKRUPTCY--
HE SAID WE HAD TO CUT COSTS--INCREASE PRODUCTION--BY ANY MEANS NECESSARY!
OUR CHEMISTS SAID--THE SILVER NITRATE LEVELS—WOULDN'T BE HARMFUL TO HUMANS--
DO I LOOK HUMAN TO YOU?!

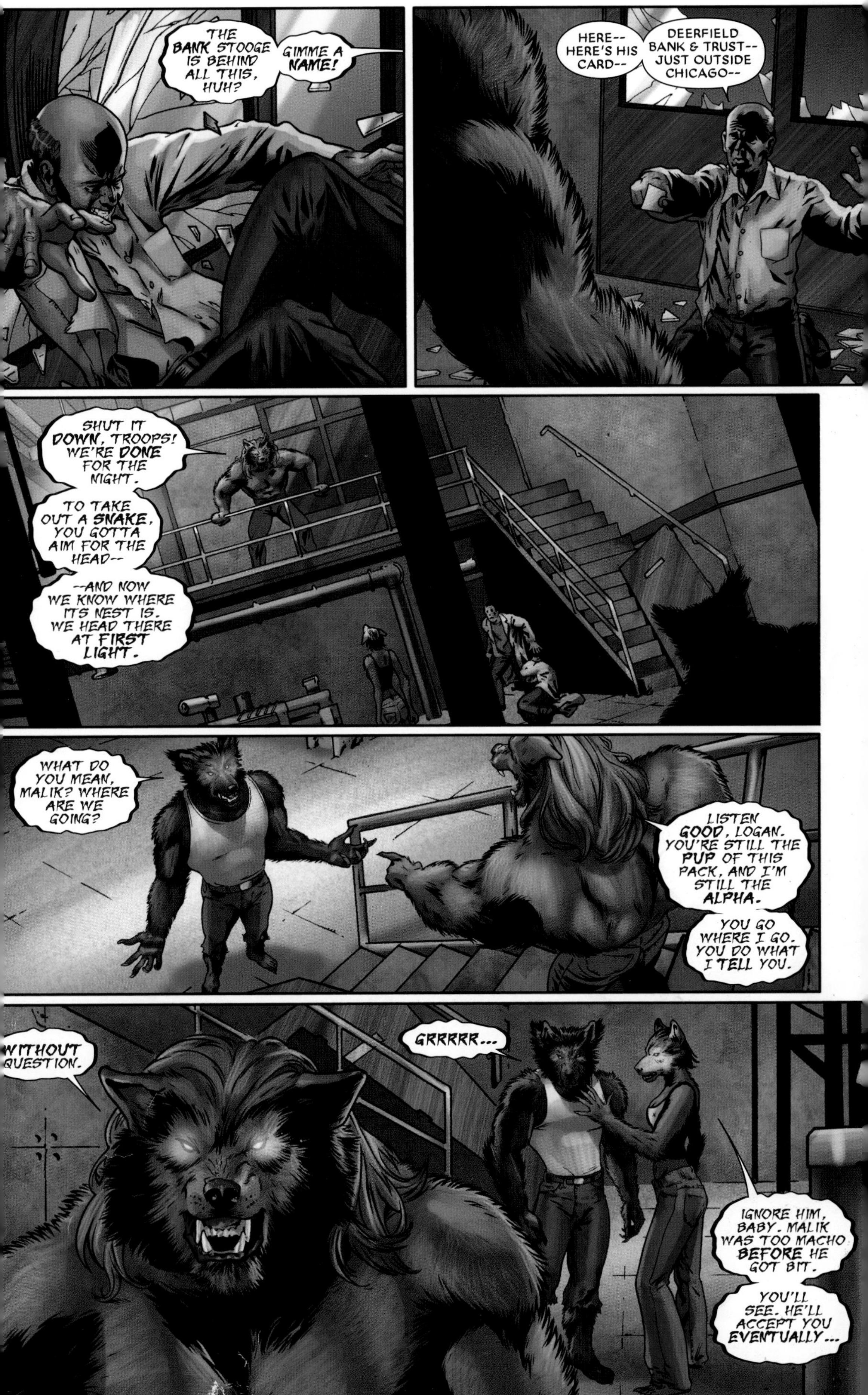
THE BANK STOOGE IS BEHIND ALL THIS, HUH?
GIMME A NAME!
HERE-- HERE'S HIS CARD--
DEERFIELD BANK & TRUST-- JUST OUTSIDE CHICAGO--
SHUT IT DOWN, TROOPS! WE'RE DONE FOR THE NIGHT.
TO TAKE OUT A SNAKE, YOU GOTTA AIM FOR THE HEAD--
--AND NOW WE KNOW WHERE ITS NEST IS. WE HEAD THERE AT FIRST LIGHT.
WHAT DO YOU MEAN, MALIK? WHERE ARE WE GOING?
LISTEN GOOD, LOGAN. YOU'RE STILL THE PUP OF THIS PACK, AND I'M STILL THE ALPHA.
YOU GO WHERE I GO. YOU DO WHAT I TELL YOU.
WITHOUT QUESTION.
GRRRRR...
IGNORE HIM, BABY. MALIK WAS TOO MACHO BEFORE HE GOT BIT.
YOU'LL SEE. HE'LL ACCEPT YOU EVENTUALLY...

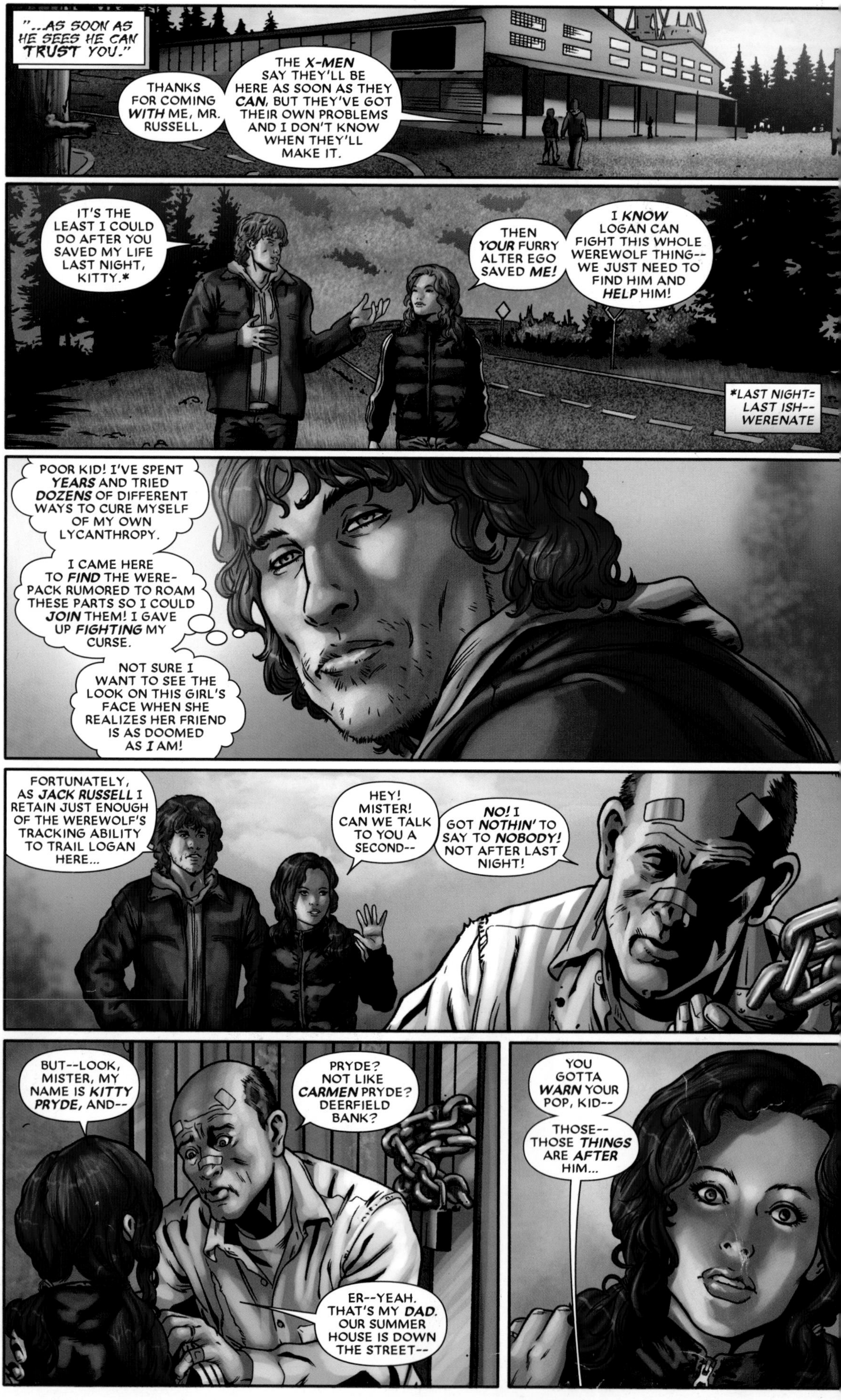
"...AS SOON AS HE SEES HE CAN TRUST YOU."
THANKS FOR COMING WITH ME, MR. RUSSELL.
THE X-MEN SAY THEY'LL BE HERE AS SOON AS THEY CAN, BUT THEY'VE GOT THEIR OWN PROBLEMS AND I DON'T KNOW WHEN THEY'LL MAKE IT.
IT'S THE LEAST I COULD DO AFTER YOU SAVED MY LIFE LAST NIGHT, KITTY.*
THEN YOUR FURRY ALTER EGO SAVED ME!
I KNOW LOGAN CAN FIGHT THIS WHOLE WEREWOLF THING--WE JUST NEED TO FIND HIM AND HELP HIM!
*LAST NIGHT= LAST ISH--WERENATE
POOR KID! I'VE SPENT YEARS AND TRIED DOZENS OF DIFFERENT WAYS TO CURE MYSELF OF MY OWN LYCANTHROPY.
I CAME HERE TO FIND THE WERE-PACK RUMORED TO ROAM THESE PARTS SO I COULD JOIN THEM! I GAVE UP FIGHTING MY CURSE.
NOT SURE I WANT TO SEE THE LOOK ON THIS GIRL'S FACE WHEN SHE REALIZES HER FRIEND IS AS DOOMED AS I AM!
FORTUNATELY, AS JACK RUSSELL I RETAIN JUST ENOUGH OF THE WEREWOLF'S TRACKING ABILITY TO TRAIL LOGAN HERE...
HEY! MISTER! CAN WE TALK TO YOU A SECOND--
NO! I GOT NOTHIN' TO SAY TO NOBODY! NOT AFTER LAST NIGHT!
BUT--LOOK, MISTER, MY NAME IS KITTY PRYDE, AND--
PRYDE? NOT LIKE CARMEN PRYDE? DEERFIELD BANK?
ER--YEAH. THAT'S MY DAD. OUR SUMMER HOUSE IS DOWN THE STREET--
YOU GOTTA WARN YOUR POP, KID--
THOSE--THOSE THINGS ARE AFTER HIM...

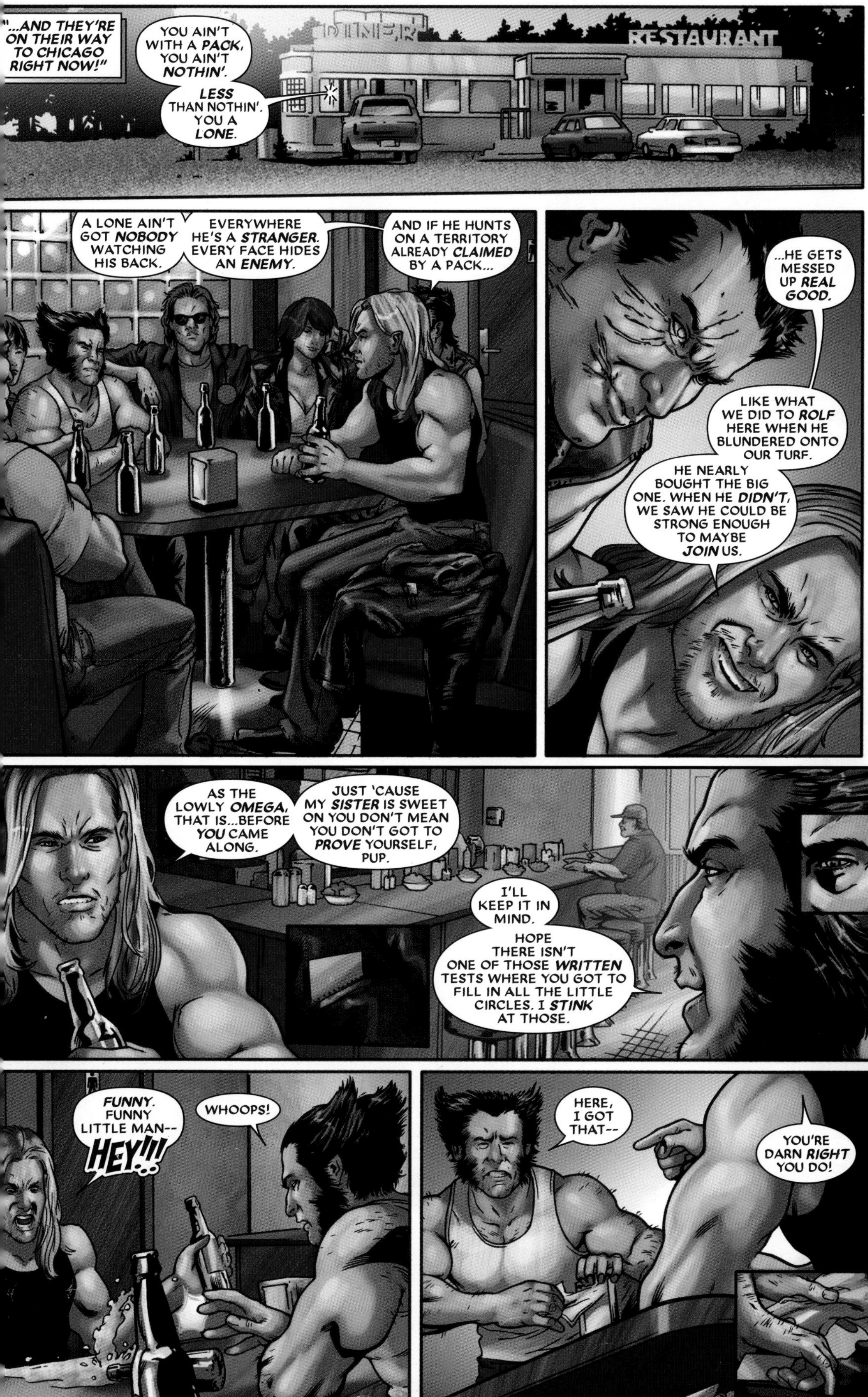
"...AND THEY'RE ON THEIR WAY TO CHICAGO RIGHT NOW!"
YOU AIN'T WITH A PACK, YOU AIN'T NOTHIN'.
LESS THAN NOTHIN'. YOU A LONE.
DINER
RESTAURANT
A LONE AIN'T GOT NOBODY WATCHING HIS BACK.
EVERYWHERE HE'S A STRANGER. EVERY FACE HIDES AN ENEMY.
AND IF HE HUNTS ON A TERRITORY ALREADY CLAIMED BY A PACK...
...HE GETS MESSED UP REAL GOOD.
LIKE WHAT WE DID TO ROLF HERE WHEN HE BLUNDERED ONTO OUR TURF.
HE NEARLY BOUGHT THE BIG ONE. WHEN HE DIDN'T, WE SAW HE COULD BE STRONG ENOUGH TO MAYBE JOIN US.
AS THE LOWLY OMEGA, THAT IS...BEFORE YOU CAME ALONG.
JUST 'CAUSE MY SISTER IS SWEET ON YOU DON'T MEAN YOU DON'T GOT TO PROVE YOURSELF, PUP.
I'LL KEEP IT IN MIND.
HOPE THERE ISN'T ONE OF THOSE WRITTEN TESTS WHERE YOU GOT TO FILL IN ALL THE LITTLE CIRCLES. I STINK AT THOSE.
FUNNY. FUNNY LITTLE MAN--
HEY!!!
WHOOPS!
HERE, I GOT THAT--
YOU'RE DARN RIGHT YOU DO!

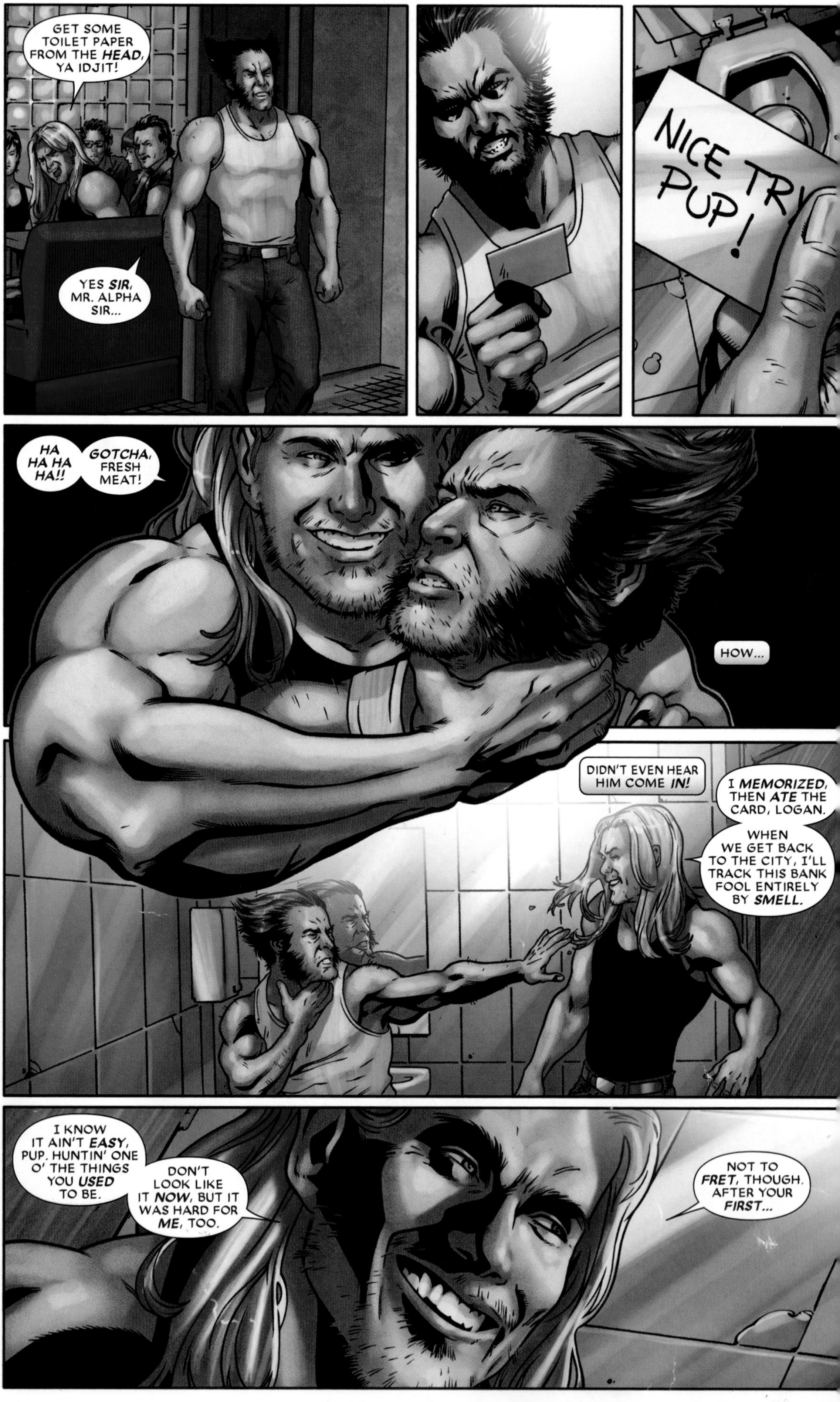
GET SOME TOILET PAPER FROM THE HEAD, YA IDJIT!
YES SIR, MR. ALPHA SIR...
NICE TRY PUP!
HA HA HA HA!!
GOTCHA, FRESH MEAT!
HOW...
DIDN'T EVEN HEAR HIM COME IN!
I MEMORIZED, THEN ATE THE CARD, LOGAN.
WHEN WE GET BACK TO THE CITY, I'LL TRACK THIS BANK FOOL ENTIRELY BY SMELL.
I KNOW IT AIN'T EASY, PUP. HUNTIN' ONE O' THE THINGS YOU USED TO BE.
DON'T LOOK LIKE IT NOW, BUT IT WAS HARD FOR ME, TOO.
NOT TO FRET, THOUGH, AFTER YOUR FIRST...

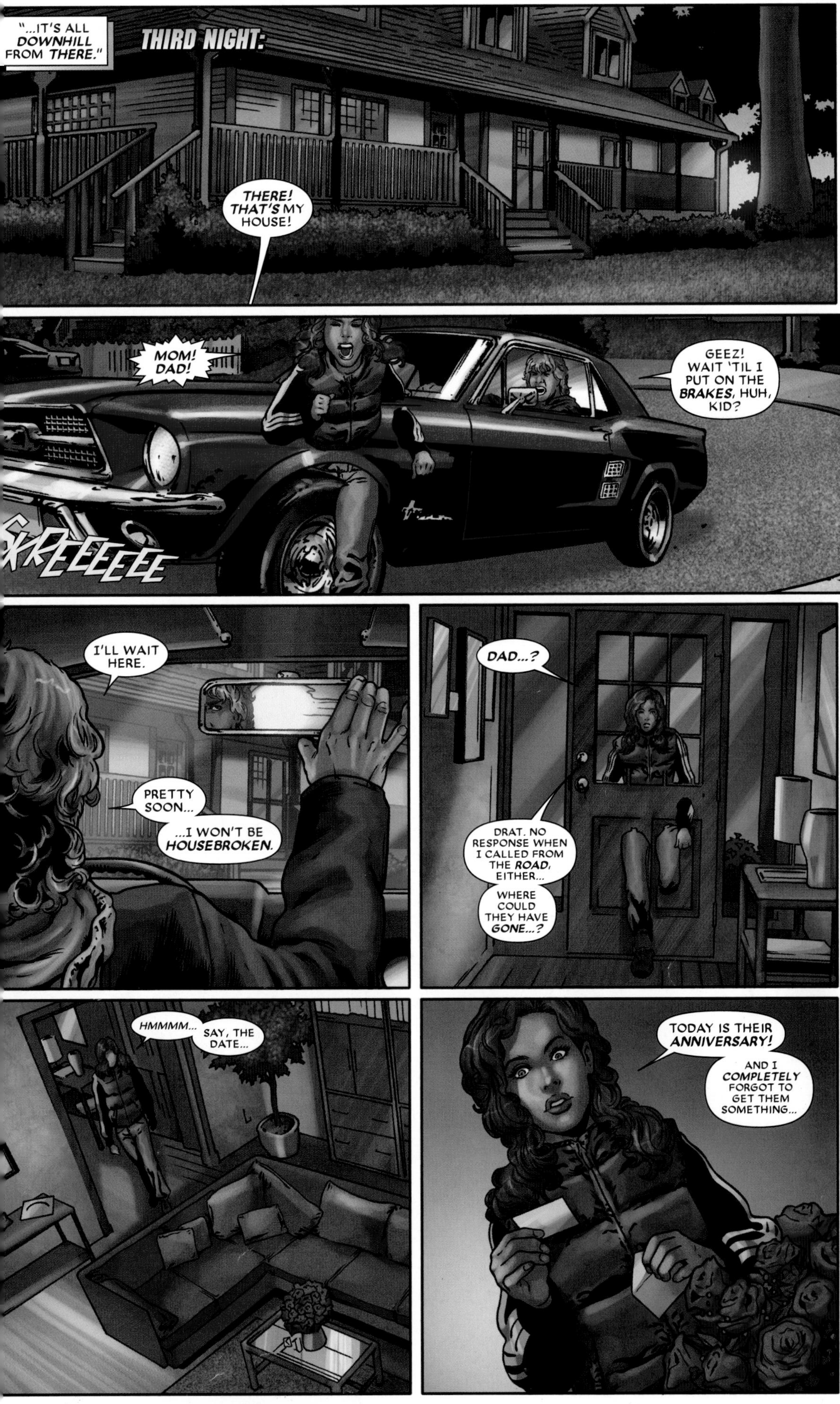

"...IT'S ALL DOWNHILL FROM THERE."
THIRD NIGHT:
THERE! THAT'S MY HOUSE!
MOM! DAD!
GEEZ! WAIT 'TIL I PUT ON THE BRAKES, HUH, KID?
SKREEEEEEE
I'LL WAIT HERE.
PRETTY SOON...
...I WON'T BE HOUSEBROKEN.
DAD...?
DRAT. NO RESPONSE WHEN I CALLED FROM THE ROAD, EITHER...
WHERE COULD THEY HAVE GONE...?
HMMMM...
SAY, THE DATE...
TODAY IS THEIR ANNIVERSARY!
AND I COMPLETELY FORGOT TO GET THEM SOMETHING...

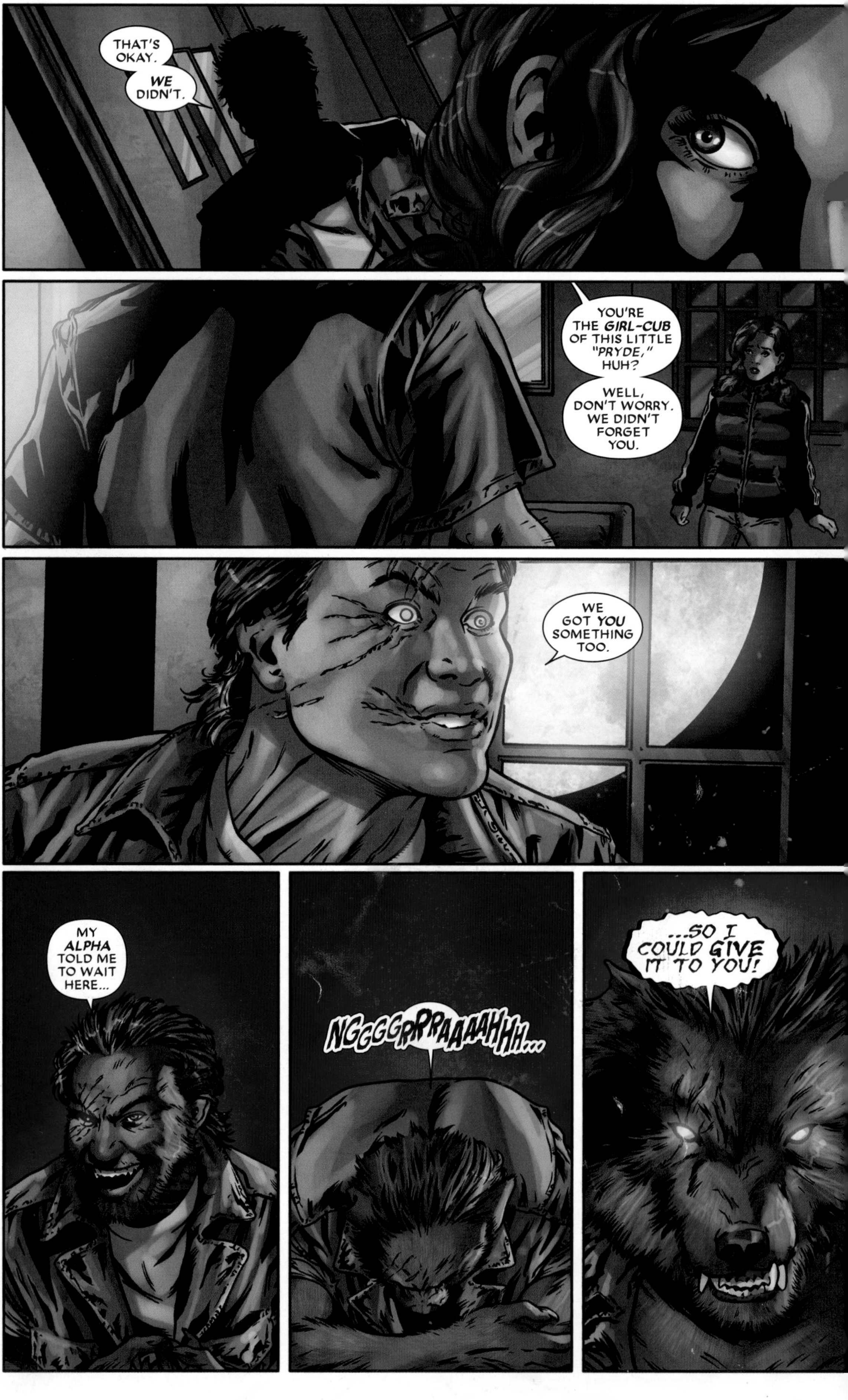
THAT'S OKAY. WE DIDN'T.
YOU'RE THE GIRL-CUB OF THIS LITTLE "PRYDE," HUH?
WELL, DON'T WORRY. WE DIDN'T FORGET YOU.
WE GOT YOU SOMETHING TOO.
MY ALPHA TOLD ME TO WAIT HERE...
NGGGGRRRAAAAHHH...
...SO I COULD GIVE IT TO YOU!

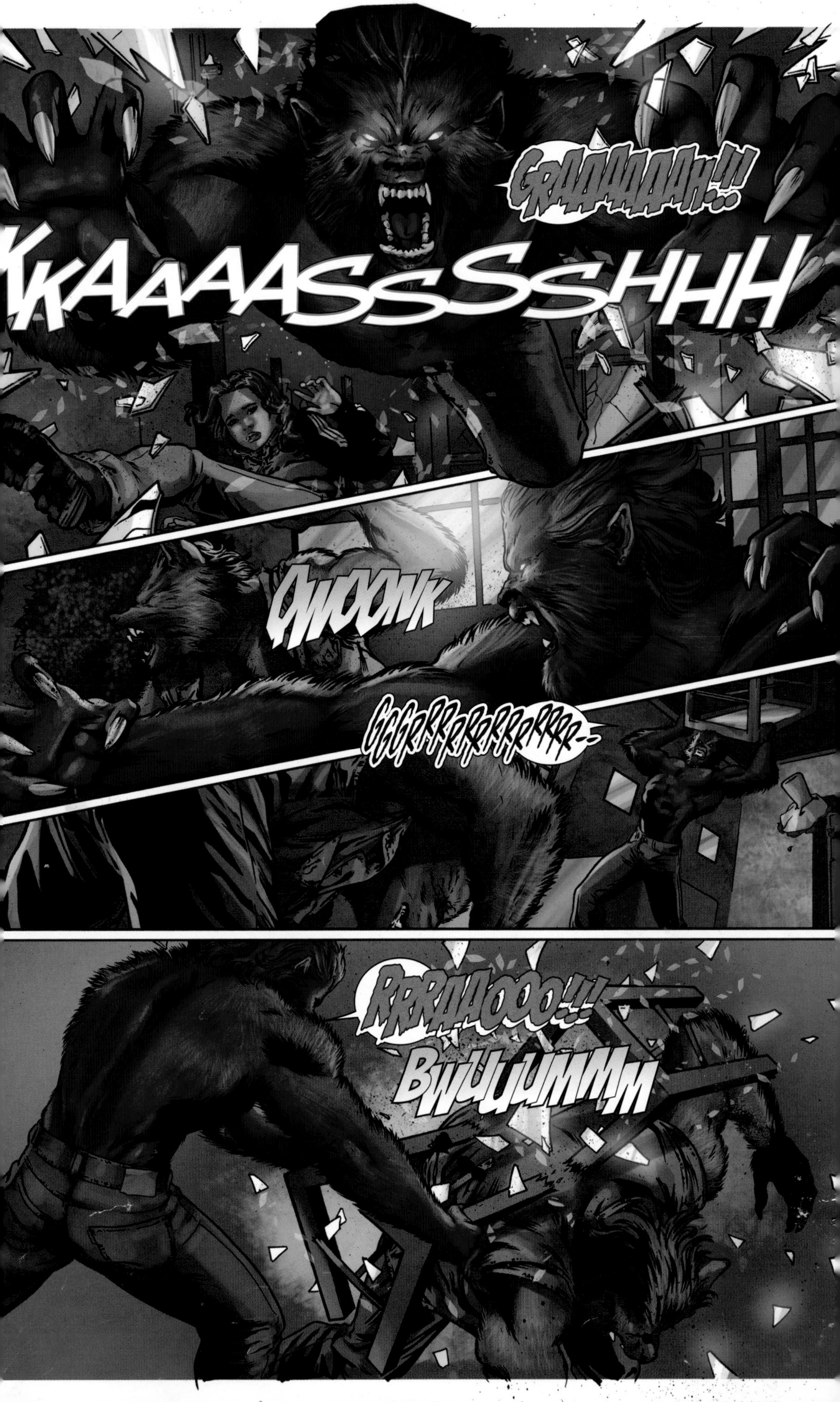
GRAAAAAAH!!!
KKAAASSSSHHH
QWOONK
GGRRRRRRRRRR-
RRRAAOOO!!!
BWUUMMMM

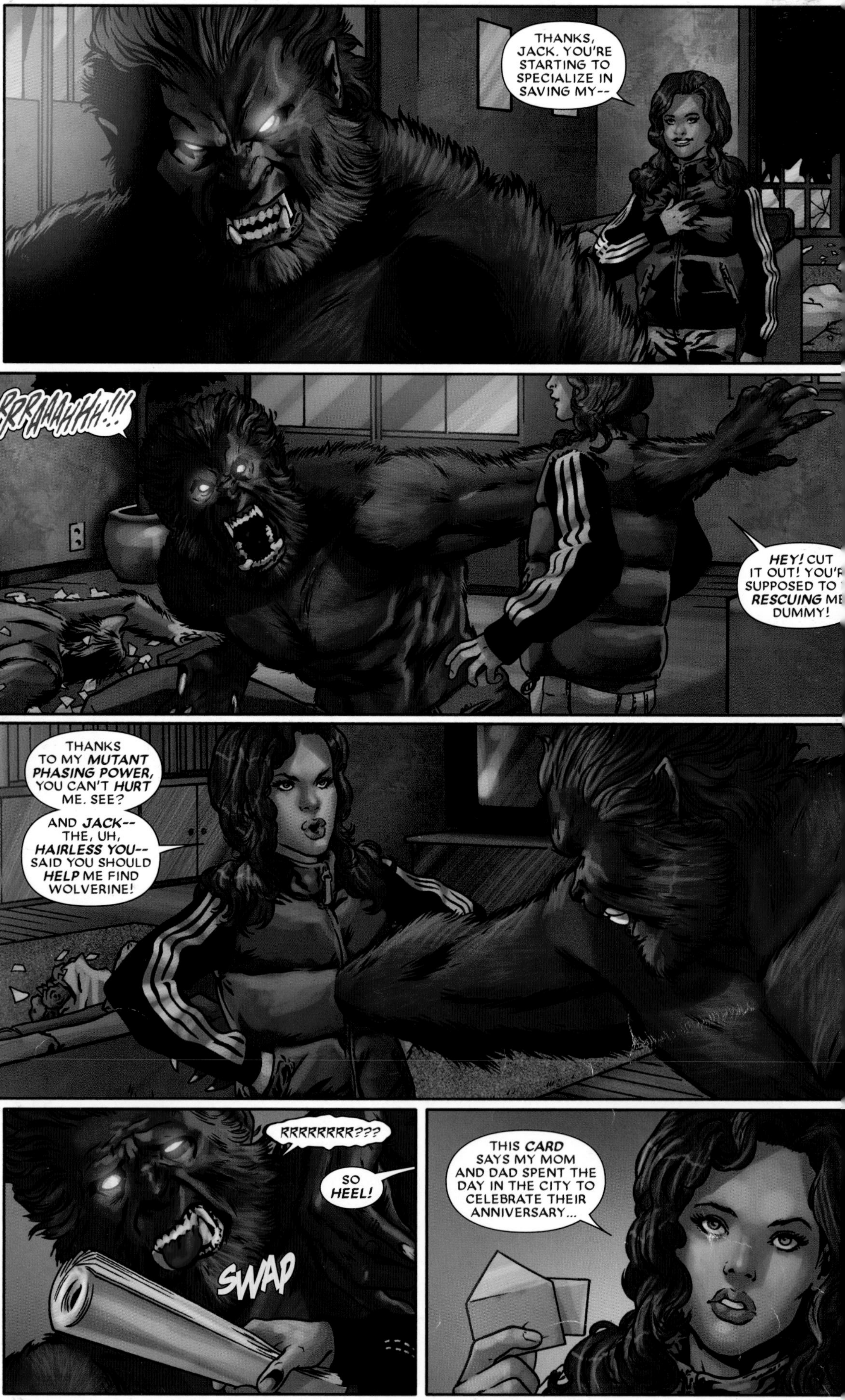
THANKS, JACK. YOU'RE STARTING TO SPECIALIZE IN SAVING MY--
RRRAAAHHH!!!
HEY! CUT IT OUT! YOU'R SUPPOSED TO RESCUING ME DUMMY!
THANKS TO MY MUTANT PHASING POWER, YOU CAN'T HURT ME. SEE?
AND JACK-- THE, UH, HAIRLESS YOU-- SAID YOU SHOULD HELP ME FIND WOLVERINE!
RRRRRRRR???
SO HEEL!
SWAP
THIS CARD SAYS MY MOM AND DAD SPENT THE DAY IN THE CITY TO CELEBRATE THEIR ANNIVERSARY...

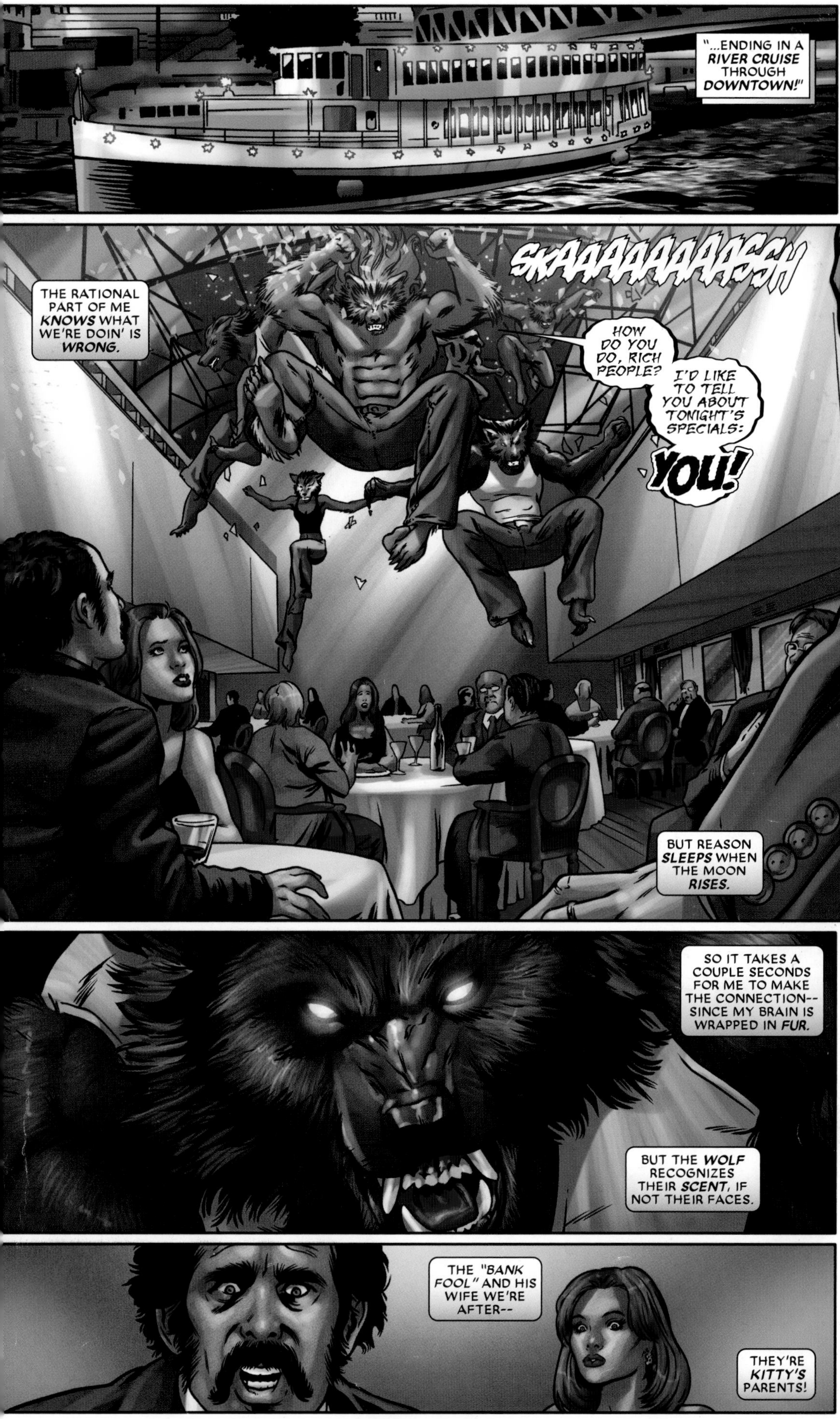
"...ENDING IN A RIVER CRUISE THROUGH DOWNTOWN!"
SKAAAAAAAASSH
THE RATIONAL PART OF ME KNOWS WHAT WE'RE DOIN' IS WRONG.
HOW DO YOU DO, RICH PEOPLE?
I'D LIKE TO TELL YOU ABOUT TONIGHT'S SPECIALS:
YOU!
BUT REASON SLEEPS WHEN THE MOON RISES.
SO IT TAKES A COUPLE SECONDS FOR ME TO MAKE THE CONNECTION-- SINCE MY BRAIN IS WRAPPED IN FUR.
BUT THE WOLF RECOGNIZES THEIR SCENT, IF NOT THEIR FACES.
THE "BANK FOOL" AND HIS WIFE WE'RE AFTER--
THEY'RE KITTY'S PARENTS!

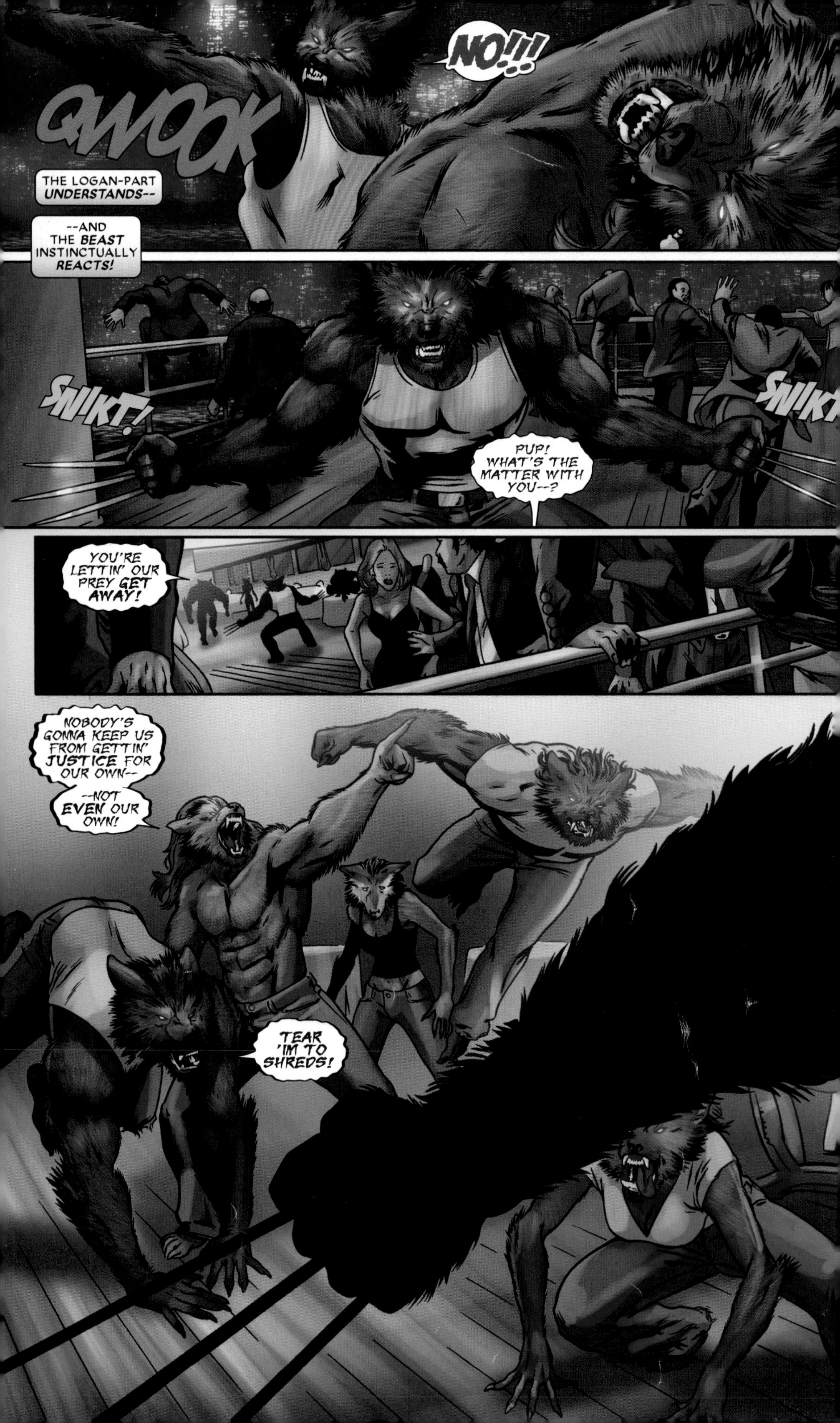
NO!!!
QWOOK
THE LOGAN-PART UNDERSTANDS--
--AND THE BEAST INSTINCTUALLY REACTS!
SNIKT!
SNIKT
PUP! WHAT'S THE MATTER WITH YOU--?
YOU'RE LETTIN' OUR PREY GET AWAY!
NOBODY'S GONNA KEEP US FROM GETTIN' JUSTICE FOR OUR OWN--
--NOT EVEN OUR OWN!
TEAR 'IM TO SHREDS!

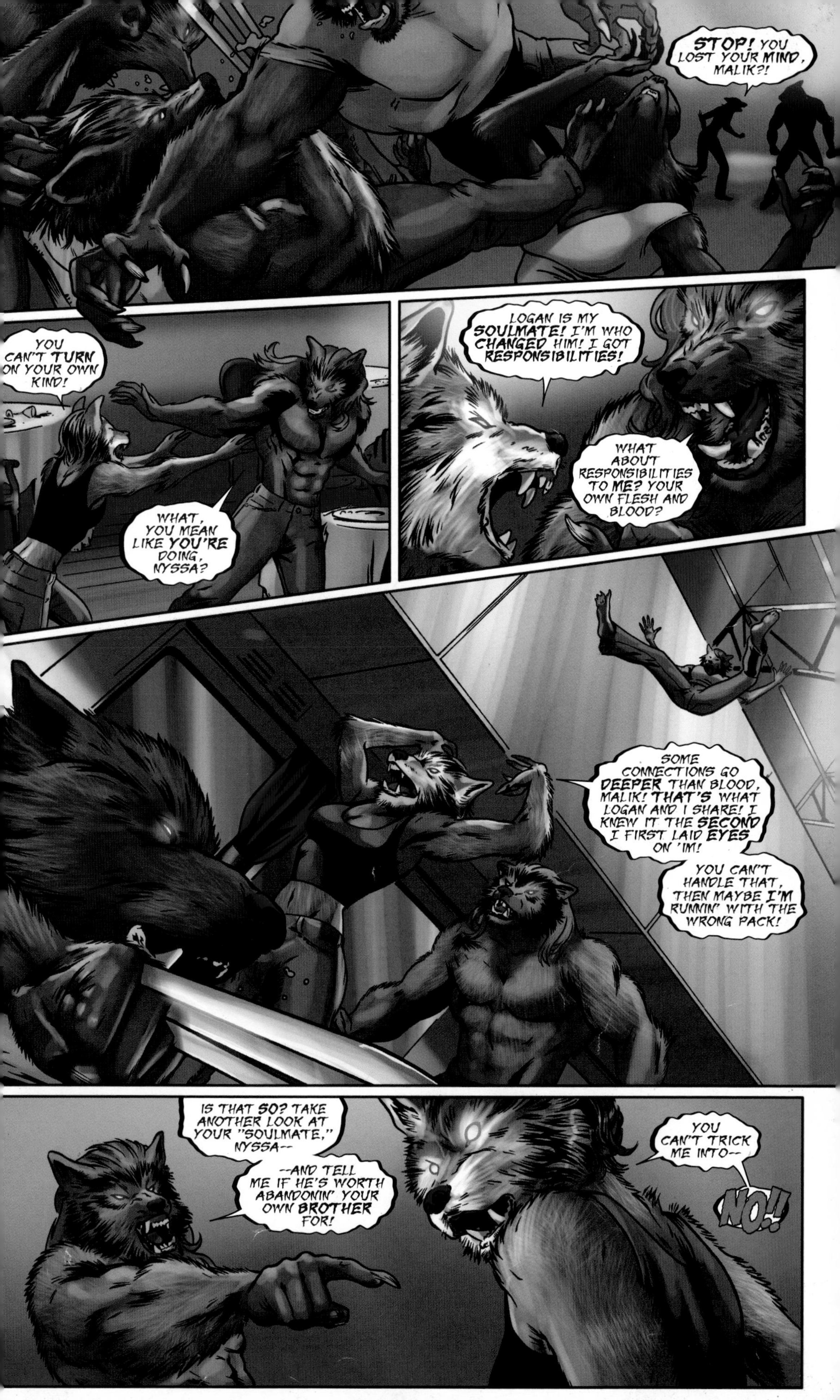
STOP! YOU LOST YOUR MIND, MALIK?!
YOU CAN'T TURN ON YOUR OWN KIND!
WHAT, YOU MEAN LIKE YOU'RE DOING, NYSSA?
LOGAN IS MY SOULMATE! I'M WHO CHANGED HIM! I GOT RESPONSIBILITIES!
WHAT ABOUT RESPONSIBILITIES TO ME? YOUR OWN FLESH AND BLOOD?
SOME CONNECTIONS GO DEEPER THAN BLOOD, MALIK! THAT'S WHAT LOGAN AND I SHARE! I KNEW IT THE SECOND I FIRST LAID EYES ON 'IM!
YOU CAN'T HANDLE THAT, THEN MAYBE I'M RUNNIN' WITH THE WRONG PACK!
IS THAT SO? TAKE ANOTHER LOOK AT YOUR "SOULMATE," NYSSA--
--AND TELL ME IF HE'S WORTH ABANDONIN' YOUR OWN BROTHER FOR!
YOU CAN'T TRICK ME INTO--
NO!!

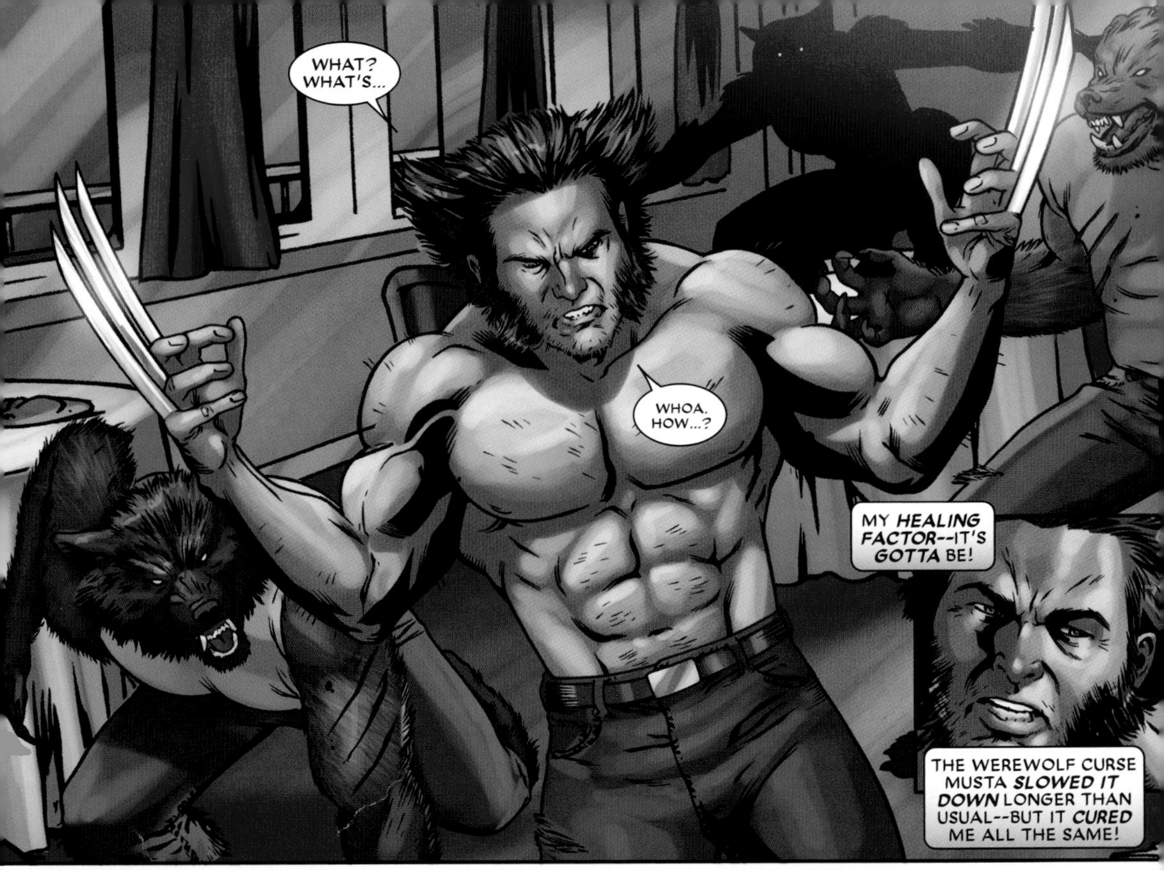
WHAT? WHAT'S...
WHOA. HOW...?
MY HEALING FACTOR--IT'S GOTTA BE!
THE WEREWOLF CURSE MUSTA SLOWED IT DOWN LONGER THAN USUAL--BUT IT CURED ME ALL THE SAME!
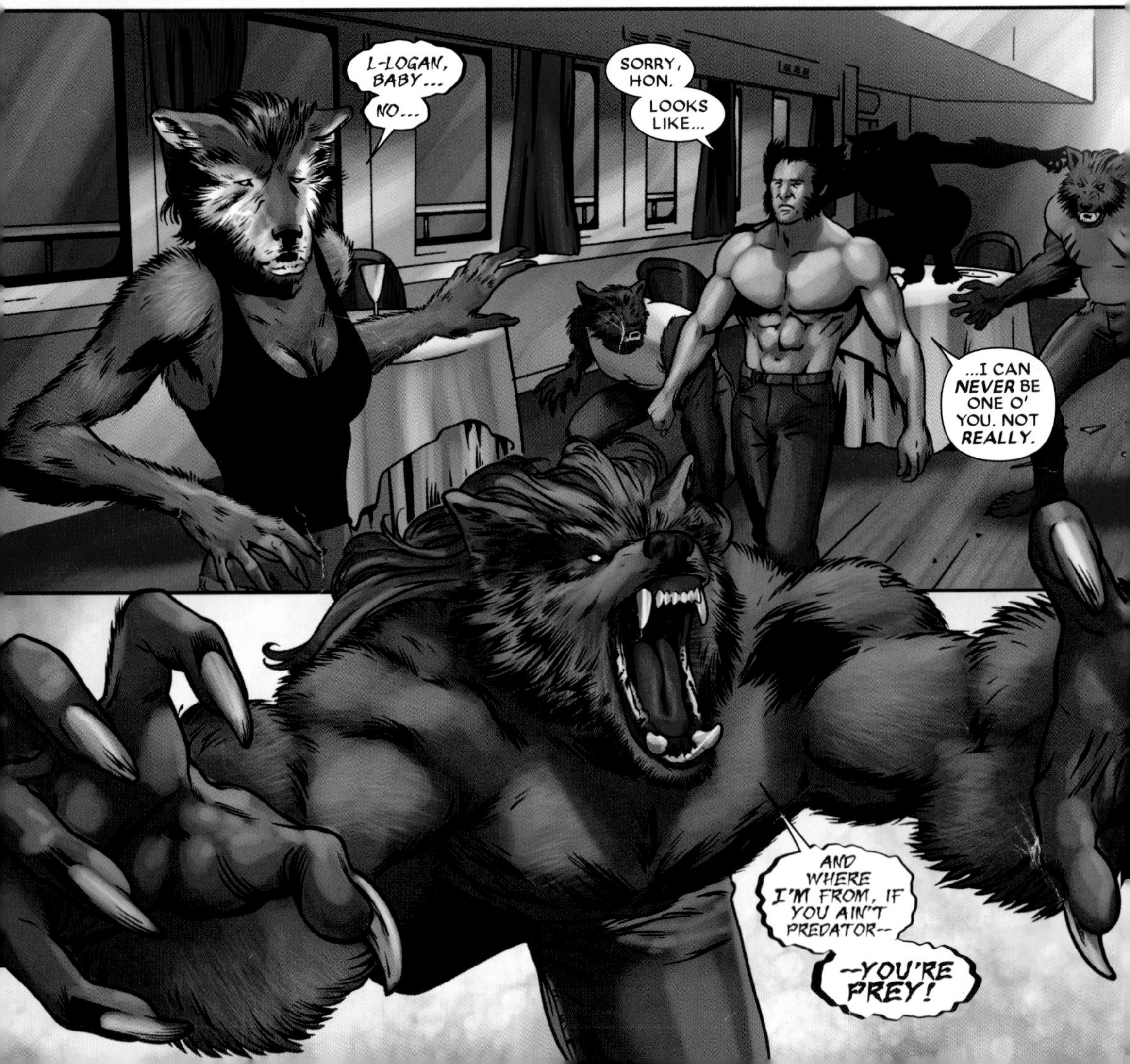
L-LOGAN, BABY...
NO...
SORRY, HON.
LOOKS LIKE...
...I CAN NEVER BE ONE O' YOU. NOT REALLY.
AND WHERE I'M FROM, IF YOU AIN'T PREDATOR--
--YOU'RE PREY!

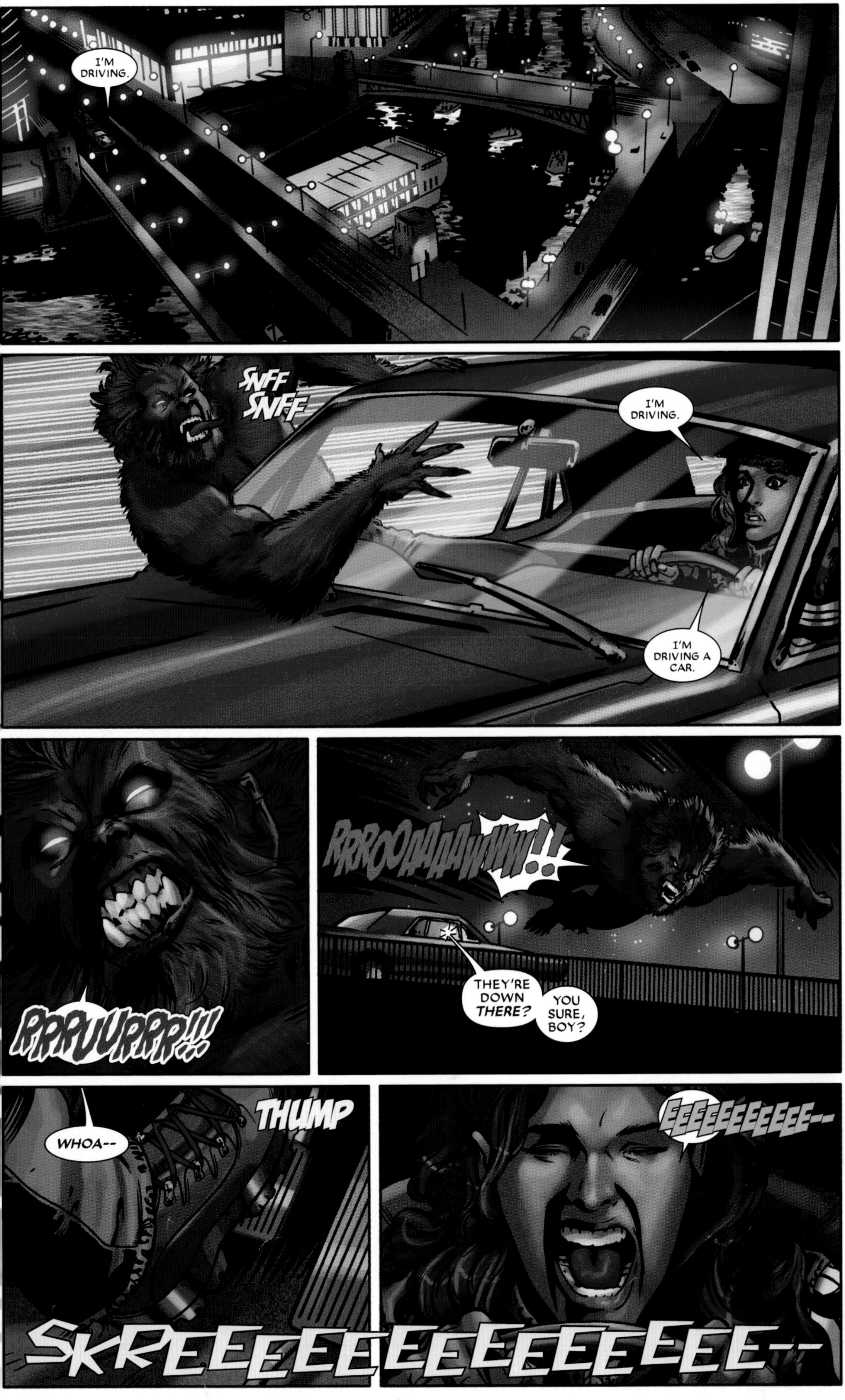
I'M DRIVING.
SNFF SNFF
I'M DRIVING.
I'M DRIVING A CAR.
RRRUURRR!!!
RRROOAAAWWW!!
THEY'RE DOWN THERE?
YOU SURE, BOY?
WHOA--
THUMP
EEEEEEEEEEE--
SKREEEEEEEEEEEEEEEE--

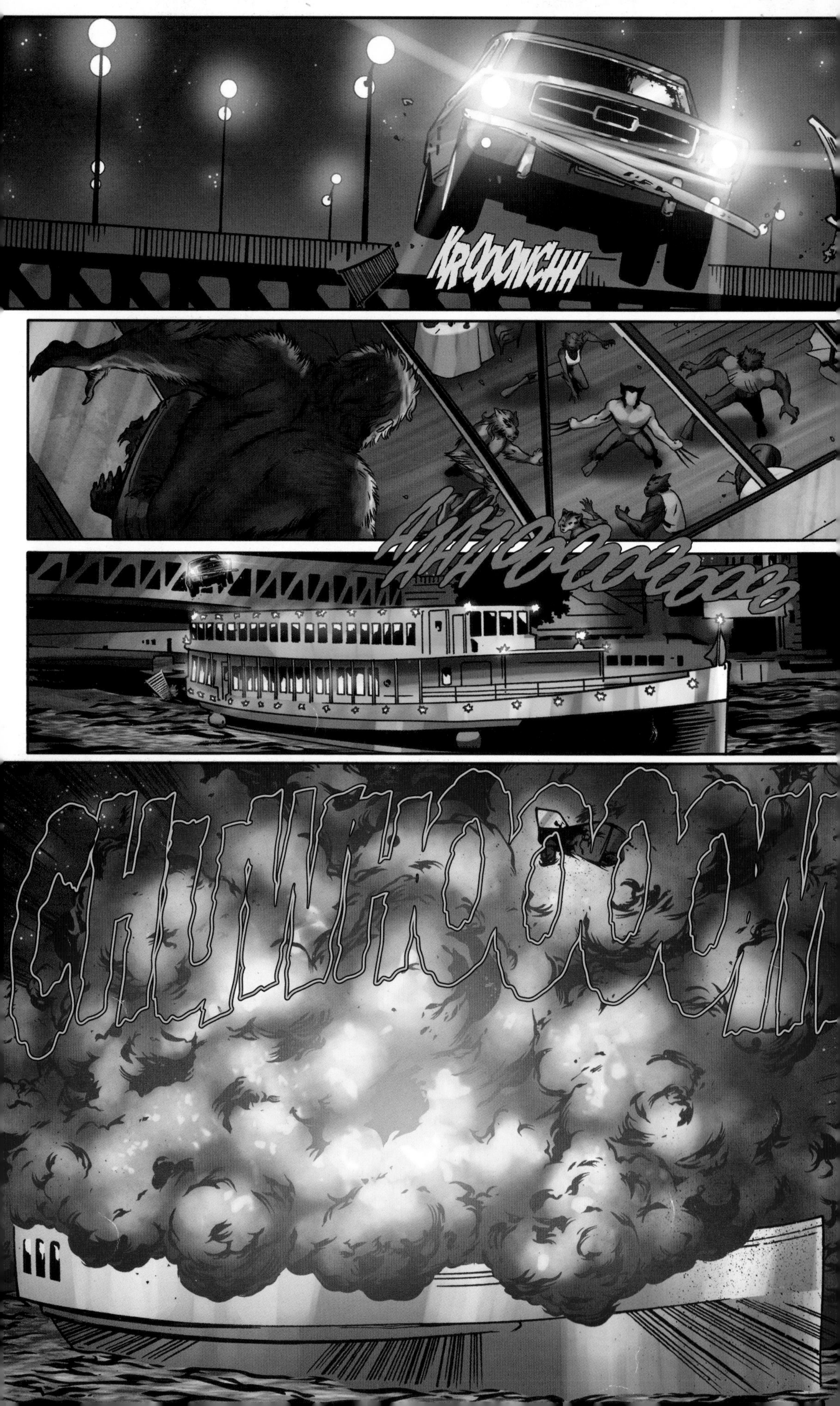
KROOOONCHH
AAAAOOOOOOOoooo
CHUMKOOOOM

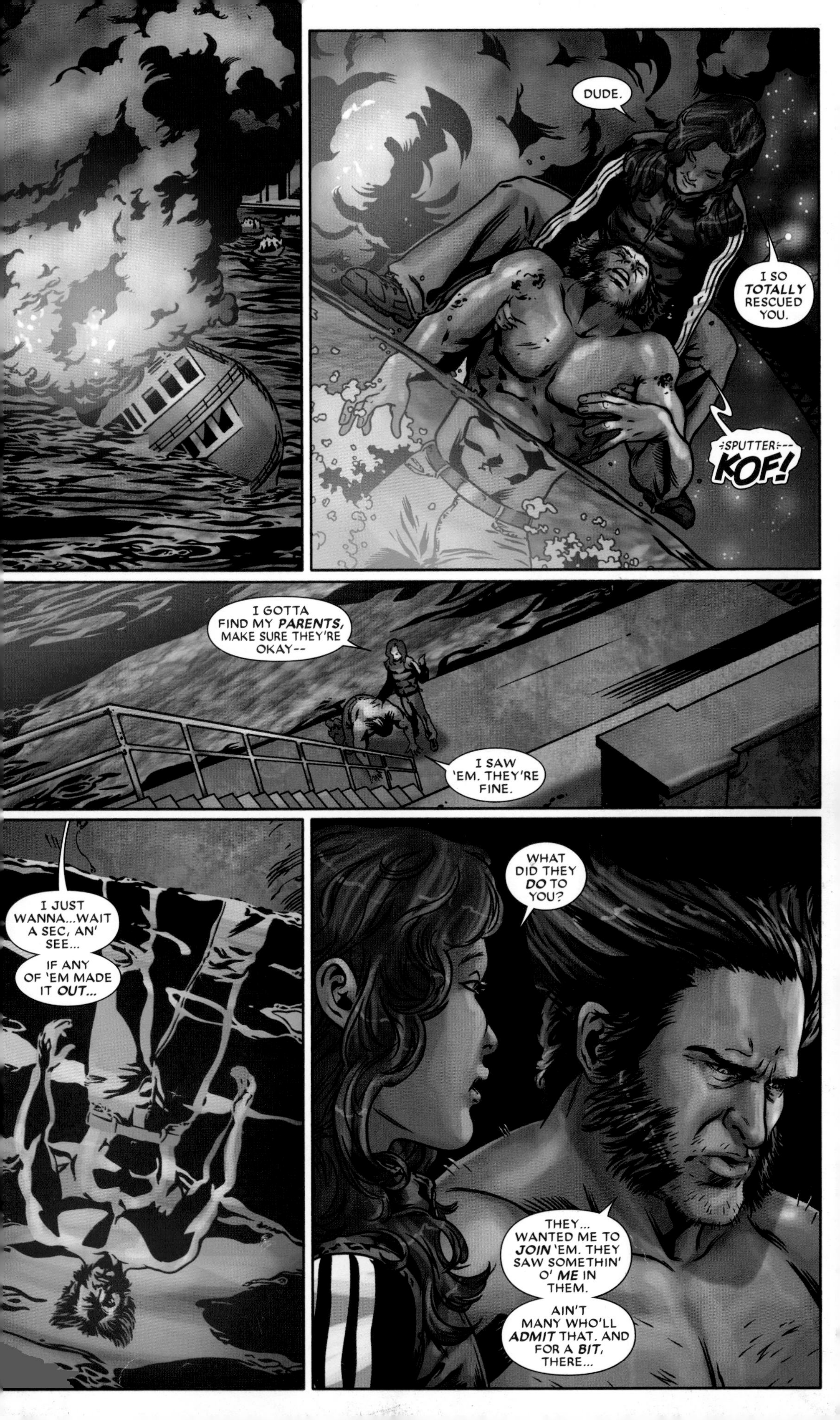
DUDE.
I SO TOTALLY RESCUED YOU.
SPUTTER-- KOF!
I GOTTA FIND MY PARENTS, MAKE SURE THEY'RE OKAY--
I SAW 'EM. THEY'RE FINE.
I JUST WANNA...WAIT A SEC, AN' SEE...
IF ANY OF 'EM MADE IT OUT...
WHAT DID THEY DO TO YOU?
THEY... WANTED ME TO JOIN 'EM. THEY SAW SOMETHIN' O' ME IN THEM.
AIN'T MANY WHO'LL ADMIT THAT. AND FOR A BIT, THERE...

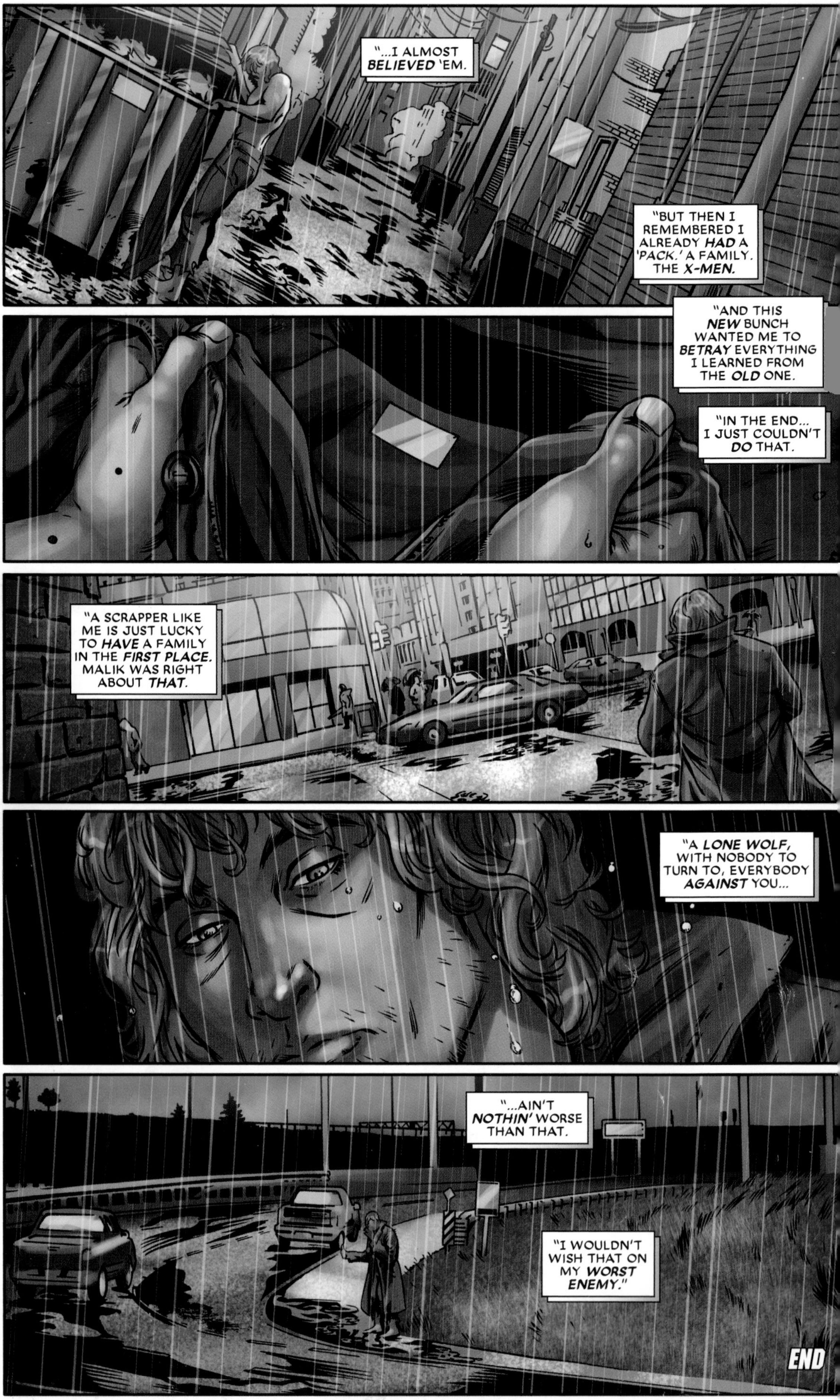
"...I ALMOST BELIEVED 'EM.
"BUT THEN I REMEMBERED I ALREADY HAD A 'PACK.' A FAMILY. THE X-MEN.
"AND THIS NEW BUNCH WANTED ME TO BETRAY EVERYTHING I LEARNED FROM THE OLD ONE.
"IN THE END... I JUST COULDN'T DO THAT.
"A SCRAPPER LIKE ME IS JUST LUCKY TO HAVE A FAMILY IN THE FIRST PLACE. MALIK WAS RIGHT ABOUT THAT.
"A LONE WOLF, WITH NOBODY TO TURN TO, EVERYBODY AGAINST YOU...
"...AIN'T NOTHIN' WORSE THAN THAT.
"I WOULDN'T WISH THAT ON MY WORST ENEMY."
END